HOW TO SURVIVE A
ZOMBIE ATTACK

By W.H. Mumfrey

The deadly serious guide to surviving zombies, aliens, robots, werewolves, vampires, and man-eating plants

Quarto is the authority on a wide range of topics.

Quarto educates, entertains and enriches the lives of our readers—enthusiasts and lovers of hands-on living.

www.quartoknows.com

© 2018 Quarto Publishing plc

First published in 2018 by QEB Publishing,
an imprint of The Quarto Group
6 Orchard Road, Suite 100
Lake Forest, CA 92630
T: +1 949 380 7510
F: +1 949 380 7575
www.QuartoKnows.com

Editor: Ellie Brough
Editorial Director: Laura Knowles
Art Director: Susi Martin
Design and picture research: Starry Dog Books

Text © Grant Murray 2018
Cover and illustrations page 58-69 illustrations © Butcher Bully 2018
All other original illustrations © Chris King 2018

A CIP record for this book is available from the Library of Congress.

ISBN 978 1 68297 384 4

9 8 7 6 5 4 3 2 1

Manufactured in Guangdong, China TT052018

MIX
Paper from responsible sources
FSC® C016973

Picture Credits
(t=top, b=bottom, l=left, r=right, c=center)

Getty: 11cr inhauscreative, 22rc Christoph Rasulis / EyeEm, 28rJohn Lund; Shutterstock: 2tr Sarawut Padungkwan, 5bl Ruslan Ivantsov, 5cr Teerawut Masawat, 6c Picsfive, 6cr Yurumi, 10cr Borkin Vadim, 10&11br&l Alhovik, 13tr A Aleksii, 13trc Demja, 13br pmmix, 13bl Best Vector Elements, 13lbc Vladvm, 15tr Nick Kinney, 15rc Cube29, 17tl canbedone, 17tl Igor Stramyk, 17lc Rvector, 17bl Paro 1, 17tr Jemastock, 17br&l svtdesign, 18tr vectortatu, 22c GoodStudio, 23tr Michael Rayback, 23rc Janis Abolins, 23bl Yuriy2012, 24tl Oleksandr Kolisnyk, 24tlc ARTSIOM ZAVADSKI, 24cl Chereliss, 24cl Hein Nouwens, 24bl VectorA, 25tr VectorPixelStar, 25cr Demja, 29tr Mirinae, 29tl Kmsdesen, 29cr JRMurray76, 29tlc Svitlana Varfolomieieva, 29br VKA, 30tc Emre Tarimcioglu, 30tr James Weston, 31tr VectorA, 31cl HuHu, 31br&l Vilingor, 35cr Maxi design, 25ct Lena graphics, 36br Warpaint, 37tr NextMars, 37br Linda Bucklin, 37bl Elena Schweitzer, 39tl Rashad Ashurov, 39tr M-SUR, 39cl Pani, 39cr Golden Shrimp, 39br johavel, 40cl Eladora, 40cr JRMurray76, 40bl LAN02, 40br GIGIBGM, 43cr design36, 46c Lario Tus, 46bl Marcos Mesa Sam Wordley, 47tl VectorA, 47cr RazorGraphix, 47bcl Korkeng, 47br Tatiana Ol'shevskaya, 48bl M-vector, 48cr johavel, 48br Alexzel, 49tl tristan tan, 49tr Iryna_Khomenko, 50bl Somyk Volodymyr, 50br Tribalium, 51tl

Serhii Borodin, 52tr LightField Studios, 55tl Teguh Mujiono, 55tr iurli, 56tr SKARIDA, 57tl DeCe, 57bl Om Yos, 57tr Serz_72, 57br Fun Way Illustration, 59tr kirill_makarov, 62tc Ociacia, 62bc Vinne, 62r Atelier Sommerland, 63tr Tatiana Shepeleva, 63br koya979, 66cl Vojtech Beran, 66cr larryrains, 66bl james weston, 66br Dmiytro, 67tr grynold, 67br aarows, 67cr Irina Adamovich, 68cr Design Collection, 68br Janis Abolins, 69tl RetroClipArt, 69cl Jamie Depledge, 69cr Andrii_M, 69bl NikhomTreeVector, 69br azem, 72c Kiselev Andrey Valerevich, 73tr tobkatrina, 73br Dm_Cherry, 74br Pushkin, 75tl johavel, 75tr lineartestpilot, 75cl In-Finity, 75rtc Mr. Luck, 75rbc VectorSun, 75br Lole, 77rtc researcher97, 77rbc Rvector, 77br DeCe, 80c kyrien, 81tl OnedayPix, 81tr Fer Gregory, 81bl Four Oaks, 82tl Four Oaks, 82tr Shaiith, 83tl illustratioz, 83cr JRMurray76, 83bl Tribalium, 83br Svjatogor, 85tl Norberthos, 85tr MicroOne, 85cr AntiMartina, 85br Pushkin, 87tl Refluo, 87tr illustratioz, 87lc VectorShop, 87cr ONYXprj, 87br Arafat Uddin, 90c Molly NZ, 91tr Z-art, 91cr Golden Shrimp, 91bl veronchick84, 91br Strilets, 92cl VectorPlotnikoff, 92rc ConstantinosZ, 92br lilac, 93tl AVA Bitter, 93tr Golden Shrimp, 94c Picsfive, 94br Yurumi; Starry Dog Books:13tl, 13tml, 50mr, 55br, 69r, 77tr; Topfoto: 27rc Fortean/Topfoto, 27bc TopFoto/Fortean.

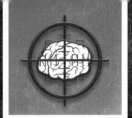

HOW TO SURVIVE A
ZOMBIE ATTACK

By W.H. Mumfrey

CONTENTS

Disclaimer

The scenarios described in this book are hypothetical. Using any of these combat techniques in real life may result in serious injuries, loss of friends, and/or imprisonment.

Dear reader,

As children, we have a natural fear of the dark. We know how important it is to close the closet in the bedroom before turning off the lights. We see the shadows on the wall for what they really are. We know exactly what the unspeakable horror is that is making the scratching sound outside our window. Yet, as we grow into adulthood, our fears are forgotten, or remembered only with a nervous chuckle. This is a mistake. We are scared of the dark for good reason: monsters are real!

Humankind has coexisted with monsters since the dawn of creation. We have known exactly what each bump-in-the-night was, ever since our hairy ancestors first swung down from the trees. Some of the world's greatest historical figures, including Albert Einstein, Amelia Earhart, Leonardo da Vinci, Charles Darwin, Jane Austen, Marie Curie, and William Shakespeare, to name but a few, all encountered, or even had to fight monsters at some time in their lives.

My name is W.H. Mumfrey and I'm a monster hunter. I have personally encountered each of the monsters described in this book and lived to tell the tales. Do not take the threat of monsters lightly. Those that do, often end up inside the digestive tract of some large, grotesque beast, rather than spending time doing the things they love, like updating their social media accounts or eating pizza. Contained within the pages of this book is all the basic information you need to not only help you survive an encounter with a monster, but also, if necessary, to vanquish it.

Let there be no mistake. The earth is in danger. The only thing standing between us and the collapse of civilization is you and your ability to survive each and every encounter with these demon spawn. The fate of our planet lies in your hands.

Keep calm and save our planet from monsters.

W.H. Mumfrey
Tasmania, 2018

Famous Monster Hunters

Charles Darwin

The great English naturalist Charles Darwin set sail on the HMS *Beagle* in 1831, not to make scientific observations that would lead to the theory of evolution, but for a well-deserved vacation. He had spent the previous year battling a plague of living dead that had resulted from bungled undergraduate experiments at Cambridge University. He thought an ocean cruise would be just what his strained nerves needed after saving Regency England from a zombie apocalypse.

Marie Curie

The famed physicist Madame Curie's invention of the X-ray machine was a happy accident, made while experimenting with radioactivity as a way to deal with a vampire epidemic sweeping through Paris.

Amelia Earhart

It was a sad day when Amelia Earhart vanished during her famous around-the-world flight, but you can bet that dragons were celebrating. As a skilled pilot, Earhart was a renowned dragon hunter. She took down many flying lizards during her famous expeditions, keeping the land and skies safe from these terrifying beasts.

Most of us don't mind dead things if they are served on a plate topped with ketchup. But when dead things start to chase you, intent on eating your brains, they soon lose their appeal. The zombie apocalypse is not for the faint-hearted.

SURVIVE A ZOMBIE APOCALYPSE

Fast facts!

ENEMY: ZOMBIE
AKA: undead, living dead, ghoul, walker, biter, infected, risen, rotter, shuffler, meat bag

ORIGIN
viral infection

WEAPONS
teeth, fingernails, smell

STRENGTHS
large groups, relentless, feels no pain, gross

WEAKNESSES
vulnerable head, rots, unintelligent

DANGER LEVEL: LOW MEDIUM HIGH EXTREME

What is a zombie?

A zombie is a person who has died and returned to life as a walking corpse. They shuffle around, slowly rotting and falling apart, while searching for living people to feed on. They are rarely invited to sleepovers or birthday parties because they smell, groan a lot, leave unsightly stains on the carpet, and try to eat the guests.

The word **"zombie"** originated in West Africa and was later used in Haiti to describe an animated corpse that had been raised by voodoo witchcraft. Zombies started appearing in movies as early as the 1930s, but the modern zombie only became a popular cultural icon in the 1960s.

Where do zombies come from?

People become zombies after being infected with the zombie virus. This virus is transmitted by way of a bite, a scratch, or contact with body fluids, such as blood, from an infected person. Once you have come into contact with the virus, it is only a matter of time before you too become a zombie.

ZOMBIE IDENTIFICATION

Don't start swinging the baseball bat too soon. Just because someone shows a few undead characteristics doesn't necessarily mean that they are a zombie. Pay close attention to the following attributes:

Vacant stare

Skin a deathly gray color

Awkward, stumbling walk

Slow zombies

Getting away from a slow zombie is like trying to run away from an old lady with a walker: not too difficult, as long as you don't do something stupid like trip, or run down a dead-end alley. Slow zombies only become a problem when you encounter a lot of them, all at once. Unfortunately, the chances of this happening are pretty high, as they tend to move around in large groups, or herds.

SLOW

GUIDE

Zombies come in two types: fast or slow. Find out which one you're facing.

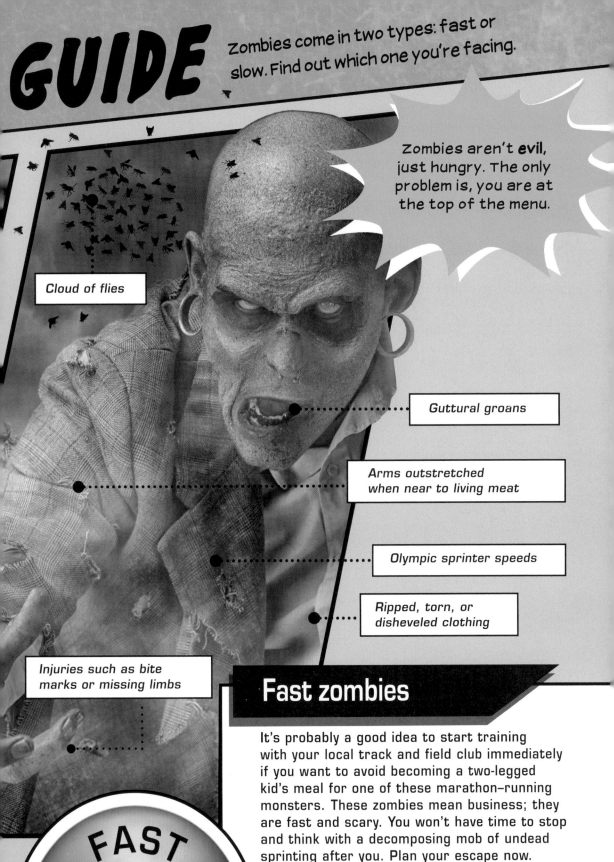

Zombies aren't **evil**, just hungry. The only problem is, you are at the top of the menu.

Cloud of flies

Guttural groans

Arms outstretched when near to living meat

Olympic sprinter speeds

Ripped, torn, or disheveled clothing

Injuries such as bite marks or missing limbs

Fast zombies

It's probably a good idea to start training with your local track and field club immediately if you want to avoid becoming a two-legged kid's meal for one of these marathon–running monsters. These zombies mean business; they are fast and scary. You won't have time to stop and think with a decomposing mob of undead sprinting after you. Plan your escape now.

FAST

ESCAPE TACTICS

You don't need to run **faster** than the mob of zombies, just faster than the person next to you...

...ng bitten by a zombie ...ot only embarrassing, ...also inconvenient. ...'ll have less than ...hours to update your ...cial media accounts ...the last time, ...fore turning into a ...mbie yourself. A few ...mple precautions could ...ve your life.

Is your home secure?

- Check that all windows and doors are locked. Nail boards over them if necessary.

- Do you have access to clean water when the taps stop working? Fill your bath now.

- Check that your garden fence is secure. Zombies can crawl through tight spaces.

- Do you have a "safe room" where you can hide if zombies get inside?

- Do you have an escape plan if things go wrong?

Stay alert

Although it may seem like fun to run around a zombie poking it with a stick, this is a mistake. While you're busy showing off to your friends, a group of undead may be staggering up behind you.

Listen up

Take out your headphones; you must pay attention to the sounds around you. Listen for groans, limbs being dragged along the floor, and weird gurgling noises. Any strange sound could mean a zombie is about to bite a chunk out of your leg.

Keep your distance

It's not always easy to tell if a body on the ground is just a body on the ground or a resting zombie. Do not approach to investigate. A zombie's dismembered body parts also remain a threat. A severed head or hand will still try to attack you.

Erect a barrier

Zombies aren't very smart. Few will think to use a door handle to enter a room, or stop if they come to the edge of a cliff. Put up a simple barrier to keep them at bay; a pile of shopping carts or old refrigerators will work well.

Be quiet, very quiet

Zombies are curious and attracted by noise. Keep talking to a minimum. Make sure you secure anything that rattles or jangles. The last thing you want is to broadcast your location, like an ice-cream truck, to every zombie in the neighborhood.

Dress for the occasion

Use body armor to protect against bites, even if it's just rolled newspaper or duct tape. You may look like a poorly-dressed knight from a medieval pageant, but you'll likely live longer.

Be noisy, very noisy

Zombies are easily distracted. If you are surrounded by a group of undead, create a diversion by throwing a rock through a windowpane. They will shuffle off to check out the commotion, giving you time to escape.

Wear some meat

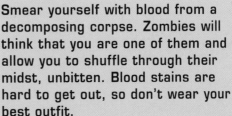

Smear yourself with blood from a decomposing corpse. Zombies will think that you are one of them and allow you to shuffle through their midst, unbitten. Blood stains are hard to get out, so don't wear your best outfit.

COMBAT

Never underestimate the danger of slow-motion monsters and never let down your guard. Zombies are like an ocean tide; they just keep coming until you are overwhelmed. When you have a hundred undead hands clutching at your ankles, remember the following combat tips:

Set a trap

Zombies aren't very smart. They can often be caught in even the simplest kinds of traps. Dig a pit trap, use some rope to make a snare, or organize a trip wire. Even a few sharp sticks pointing in the right direction can entangle hapless zombies.

Headshot

The only effective way to "kill" a zombie is to destroy what's left of its brain. It's really up to your own imagination how you do this, but be warned, it's not as easy as you think. Just try throwing a basketball through a hoop while a pack of wild dogs is racing toward you—what appears to be easy under normal circumstances suddenly becomes almost impossible when under pressure.

Pruning

While destroying its brain is the only way to stop a zombie in its tracks, aiming for other parts of its body can have the effect of slowing it down. Try climbing upstairs without using your legs, or wriggling from your living room to the kitchen, and you'll see why. Use this extra time to escape.

Follow the leader

Ring the bell on your bicycle or bang on a trash can lid to attract the attention of as many zombies as you can. Now lead them into your local quarry or sports field. When they are all inside, simply slip past them and lock the gates. Most zombies only shuffle, so it will be a very slow chase. Make sure you thoroughly check your exit before you begin and never, ever try this with fast zombies; they will catch you and they will eat you.

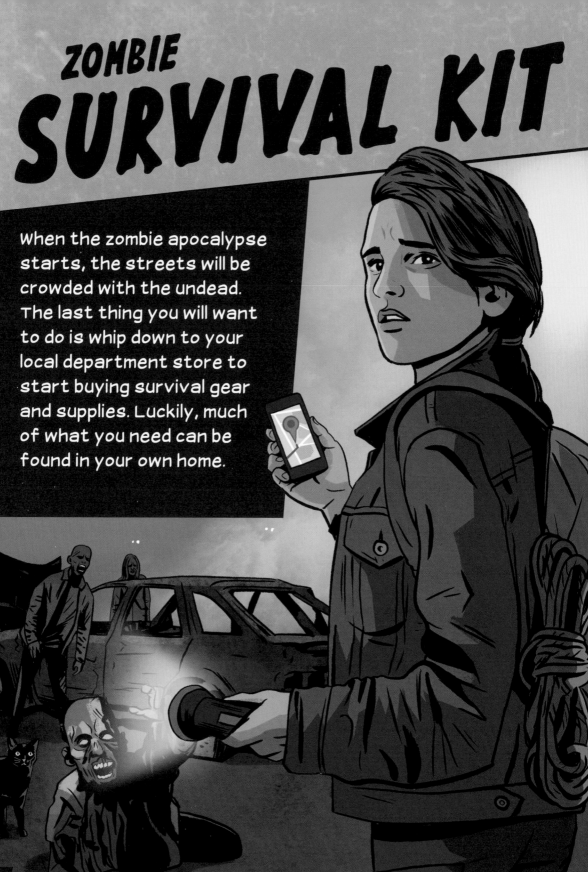

ZOMBIE
SURVIVAL KIT

When the zombie apocalypse starts, the streets will be crowded with the undead. The last thing you will want to do is whip down to your local department store to start buying survival gear and supplies. Luckily, much of what you need can be found in your own home.

Map and compass

When the Internet goes down during a zombie apocalypse, there will be no more satellite navigation. Make sure your map reading skills are up to scratch; you'll need to know the best routes out of town.

Sunglasses

Apart from keeping the sun out of your eyes at pivotal moments, they also keep zombie splatter out too. Bonus: you'll look cool, but that shouldn't be your main priority.

Backpack

Not only are backpacks handy for carrying all your survival gear, but also for stowing food when you're out foraging through abandoned supermarkets and homes.

Immunization

Are your vaccinations up to date? It may not be the zombies that kill you, but tetanus from the nail you just stepped on while running away from them.

Flashlight

There's only one thing worse than being chased by zombies and that is being chased by zombies in the dark. Make sure you carry a flashlight and spare batteries.

ARE YOU AT RISK?

Danger doesn't always arrive unexpectedly. Sometimes there are telltale signs that indicate all is not well. Assess your current state of danger by asking yourself the following questions:

Quiz

1 Are there reputable **news reports** on TV or in your social media feed about people randomly biting other people?

2 Have you noticed your neighbors **loading their cars** with boxes of food and personal belongings and driving off unexpectedly?

3 Have you seen people **lumbering around** the streets, surrounded by clouds of flies and snarling at passers-by?

4 Have you caught a whiff of something that smells like two-week-old **roadkill**, but you're not near a road?

5 Is your teacher looking deader than usual or starting to **bite students**?

6 Is the person you just bumped into **moaning** and **staggering** toward you with their arms outstretched, and a hungry expression on what's left of their face?

7 Do you hear **automatic weapon fire**, planes crashing, and the guttural moans of a hundred or more undead staggering up your street?

8 Do you hear the sound of **undead feet being dragged** up the hallway toward your room?

9 Can you hear the sound of cold, dead **fingernails scratching** at your door?

10 Does the hand suddenly grasping your shoulder feel like the **cold, bony fingers** of the skeleton from your school science room?

Risk factor

Add up your score. Where did you fall on the "at risk" scale?

0–1 There could be a normal explanation. Stay alert for developments.

2–4 Something is clearly desperately wrong.

5–6 Get out of town now before it's too late.

7–8 Arm yourself; you're in for the fight of your life.

9–10 Fight first, ask questions later. You're in a life-and-death situation.

The story of Little Red Riding Hood warns us of the dangers of talking to wolves. This is especially true when it comes to werewolves. You won't want to pat these not-so-cuddly canines; they're all fur, fangs, and fury.

SURVIVE A WEREWOLF ATTACK

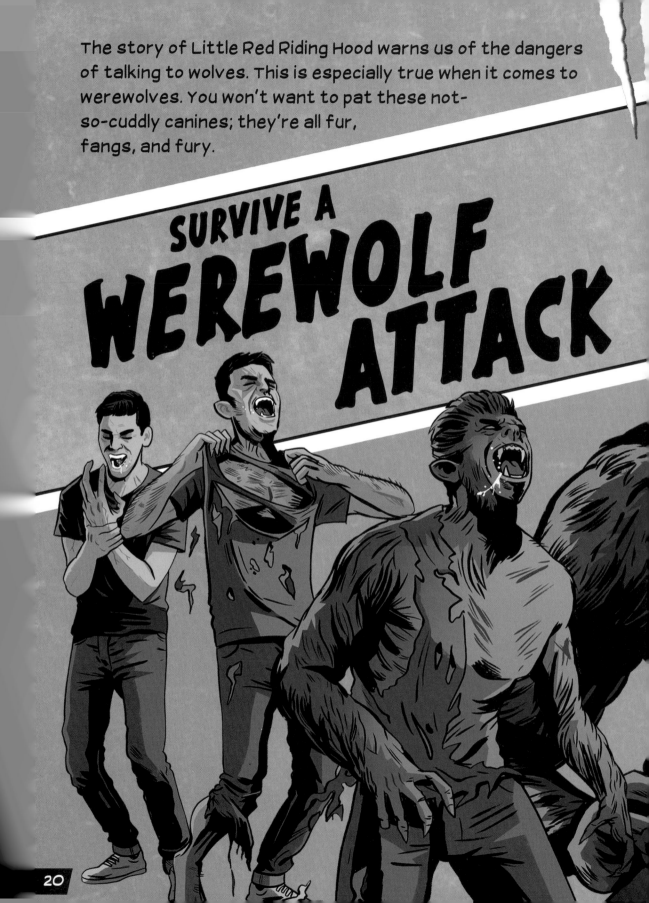

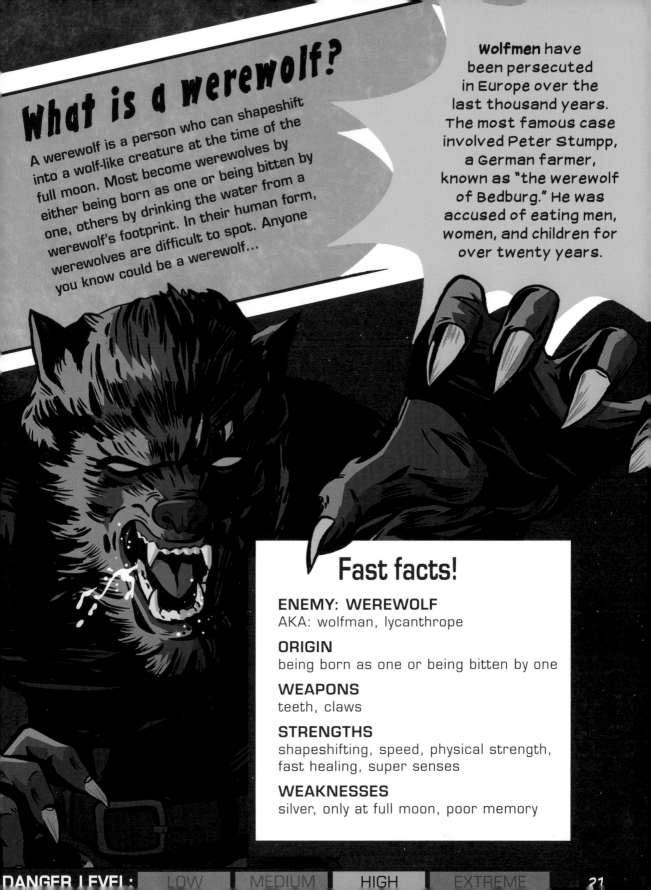

What is a werewolf?

A werewolf is a person who can shapeshift into a wolf-like creature at the time of the full moon. Most become werewolves by either being born as one or being bitten by one, others by drinking the water from a werewolf's footprint. In their human form, werewolves are difficult to spot. Anyone you know could be a werewolf...

Wolfmen have been persecuted in Europe over the last thousand years. The most famous case involved Peter Stumpp, a German farmer, known as "the werewolf of Bedburg." He was accused of eating men, women, and children for over twenty years.

Fast facts!

ENEMY: WEREWOLF
AKA: wolfman, lycanthrope

ORIGIN
being born as one or being bitten by one

WEAPONS
teeth, claws

STRENGTHS
shapeshifting, speed, physical strength, fast healing, super senses

WEAKNESSES
silver, only at full moon, poor memory

WEREWOLF IDENTIFICATION

You'll know a werewolf if you see one; they are not difficult to identify. Best practice is to identify your werewolf before the full moon. That way you will be prepared.

Human eyes

Large canine teeth

Breath that smells like fresh meat

Excessively hairy

Sharp, "claw-lik[e]" fingernails

Larger than a full-grown man

Spot a werewolf in human form

Werewolves in their human form can easily walk unnoticed down a crowded street. With a trained eye, however, you will notice some telltale signs.

• Is the person excessively hairy?

• When you shine a flashlight in their eyes, do they reflect like a dog's eyes?

• Does the person have a monobrow (where two eyebrows meet in the middle to look like a singe eyebrow)?

• When wet, do they smell a little like a wet dog?

ESCAPE TACTICS

The words of Benjamin Franklin, "an ounce of prevention is worth a pound of cure," are never more true than when dealing with werewolves. Avoiding werewolves is not too difficult; surviving an encounter with one is a little more tricky.

Full moon

Avoid traveling during a full moon. Werewolves are most active during this period. A full moon lasts about three or four days and occurs approximately once every four weeks. Mark these dates in your diary, or on your calendar, and stay at home.

Hide your tracks

Werewolves are very good at hunting and can track your scent just like a bloodhound. Cover your scent by walking in water, changing direction often, and staying in crowds as much as possible to help mask your odor.

Public transport

If a werewolf starts chasing you while you are in town, jump on a bus or train. Werewolves have superhuman strength and endurance, but they're unlikely to outrun public transport. Always buy a ticket first.

Trust your instincts

If you feel like you are being followed, you probably are. Werewolves are cunning and just because you can't see a werewolf, doesn't mean that you aren't being watched by one right now. Slowly scan your surroundings and take immediate action if you sense danger.

Last resort

Once a werewolf returns to its human form, it will not remember anything about what happened when it was in its werewolf form. Most werewolves do not want to be werewolves. Helping to control its condition while in its human form is a good way of preventing carnage during its werewolf stage. Destroying a werewolf is always a last resort.

WEREWOLF
SURVIVAL KIT

If you're not afraid of the big, bad wolf, you should be. Improve your chances of survival by carrying these items:

Silver

Anything made from silver will burn a werewolf's skin upon contact.

Catapult

Use this hand-held device to propel small pieces of silver at a werewolf.

Spear

Use duct tape to attach a silver knife or fork to the end of a stick to make a spear.

Wolf's bane

Werewolves are not fond of this common plant from the Northern Hemisphere. Do not rely on this if cornered.

Flashlight

Use a flashlight to locate a werewolf's eyes shining in the dead of night.

COMBAT

Werewolves are fast, strong, and have superhuman senses of sight and smell. Your best hope is to avoid a fight, but if cornered, remember these tips:

Silver bullet

The traditional way to kill a werewolf is with a silver bullet. But how many of us have silver bullets lying around, or a gun to fire them with? Luckily, werewolves don't like any kind of silver: silver cutlery, candelabras, or jewelry will work in a fix.

Regeneration

Werewolves have amazing healing powers and can regenerate wounds and limbs very quickly. The only time they won't heal themselves is when they are dead. Make sure you achieve this goal or have a good escape plan. Wounding a werewolf only makes it very, very angry.

Chop, chop

The Queen of Hearts gave good advice in *Alice's Adventures in Wonderland*, when she said, "Off with their heads!" Although this is an effective way to kill a werewolf, getting close enough to do so is extremely hazardous.

Tidy up

Werewolves return to their human form once they have been killed. You will now face the problem of trying to explain to the police why there is a dead body at your feet. Avoid this situation by avoiding werewolves.

25

Bigfoot's huge feet aren't the only thing you need to worry about—everything else about Bigfoot is big as well. Bigfoot is huge, smelly, and, more often than not, angry. If you want to stay off the menu, you had better start training now.

SURVIVE A BIGFOOT ABDUCTION

Fast facts!

ENEMY: BIGFOOT
AKA: sasquatch, yeti, abominable snowman, yowie, barmanou

ORIGIN
wild forests and mountains

WEAPONS
teeth, claws

STRENGTHS
physical strength, stealth, speed

WEAKNESSES
dim-witted, scares easily, solitary

DANGER LEVEL: | LOW | MEDIUM | HIGH | EXTREME

What is Bigfoot?

This huge, bipedal, ape-like creature has been sighted throughout the world, from the outback deserts of Australia, to the frozen Himalayan Mountains in Nepal. Bigfoot's feet are, as you may well imagine, big, measuring up to 24 inches long and 8 inches wide.

Bigfoot   Human

Caught on camera

The most famous film of Bigfoot was shot in 1967. Two friends, Roger Patterson and Robert Gimlin, were on a Bigfoot hunting expedition in Northern California, USA. They saw a large, hairy, ape-like figure walking away from them. The minute of footage that Patterson took on that day is equivalent in fame to the famous Loch Ness Monster photo, shot in Scotland in 1934.

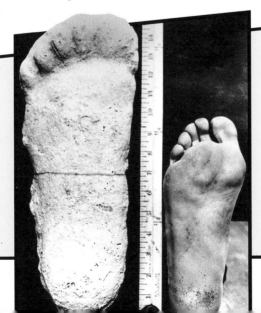

Footprints

When in the wild, always be on the lookout for footprints left in the dirt or snow. These tracks will let you know what animals have been in the vicinity recently, including Bigfoot. If the footprint is fresh, be on your guard: Bigfoot is about.

BIGFOOT

It's easy to spot Bigfoot; here's what you need to look out for.

IDENTIFICATION

Identifying Bigfoot will not be a challenge. He's like nothing else you will ever encounter in the wild, except maybe someone in a giant gorilla suit. If you think you may have trouble, look for the following:

Large, sloping forehead

Prominent brow ridge

Large eyes

6–10 feet tall

Hairy

Muscular body

Bipedal (stands on two legs)

Strong, unpleasant smell

BIGFOOT SURVIVAL KIT

If you are out exploring the wild, make sure you have the following gear in your backpack; you just never know when you may need it.

A pet dog

Dogs have excellent senses and can often smell or hear danger a long time before you can. Bigfoot doesn't like dogs and will stay clear.

Binoculars

It's better to spot Bigfoot from a distance so you'll have a headstart for when you need to run away.

Harmonica

Play a musical instrument as you walk in the forest, or at least whistle a tune. Bigfoot is scared of strangers so will avoid unfamiliar sounds.

Snacks

Bigfoot loves snacks. Keep a ready supply in your backpack and resist the urge to eat them.

ESCAPE TACTICS

We can't avoid the inevitable, but we can be prepared for it. If you're hiking in Bigfoot country, remember the following:

Avoid his territory

Bigfoot lives in remote wilderness areas, although he's been known to travel to other regions. He can be found in deep, dark forests or in mountains. He's rarely seen in towns.

Travel in a group

Bigfoot is less likely to attack you if you are traveling with a number of other people. If Bigfoot hears a big group coming, he will probably hide and wait for you to pass.

Carry snacks

Bigfoot will only attack you if he feels threatened or hungry. Either way, the situation is never good. If cornered, throwing some food into the bushes may distract him long enough for you to escape.

COMBAT

If you find yourself fighting an enraged beast the size of a refrigerator, remember the following tips:

Avert your gaze

Many animals interpret looking directly in their eyes as a hostile gesture. Don't look Bigfoot directly in his eyes; it will only make him angry and more likely to kill you.

Shine a light

If you meet Bigfoot at night, shine a flashlight in his eyes; the dazzling light will temporarily distract him, giving you time to escape. It will also momentarily damage his night vision, making it more difficult for him to give chase.

Sticks and stones

Throw whatever you have handy at Bigfoot. You never know your luck; you might hit him where it hurts—his nose—giving you a chance to run away while he sees to his injuries.

Trap it

Bigfoot can be trapped just like any other beast. You will need to be sneaky, though, as Bigfoot is wary of things which show signs of human tampering. That's how he has survived so long. A pit trap is a good Bigfoot defense. Make sure it's deep enough so he can't climb back out.

A poke in the eye

If worst comes to worst and you find yourself in a to-the-death bear hug with Bigfoot, remember the most vulnerable parts of Bigfoot's body at close range are his eyes. Use your fingers or thumbs to poke, scratch, or gouge until he lets go. Run for safety as fast as you can; Bigfoot will now be very, very annoyed.

Little green men from Mars may not appear to be too much of a threat in today's troubled world, but give these extraterrestrial creatures laser blasters and heat rays and it's quite a different story.

SURVIVE AN
ALIEN INVASION

Fast facts!

ENEMY: ALIEN
AKA: extraterrestrial, little green man, space being, gray, transformer, bug, blob, Martian, parasitic alien

ORIGIN
outer space

WEAPONS
laser blaster, heat ray, death ray, phaser, pulse gun, particle beam, plasma gun

STRENGTHS
superior technologies, warp speeds, cloaking devices

WEAKNESSES
Earth's microbes, human ingenuity and perseverance

DANGER LEVEL: LOW   MEDIUM   HIGH   EXTREME

What is an alien?

An alien is a creature from somewhere other than Earth. They come in a variety of shapes and sizes; some are as small as bacteria and others tower above city skyscrapers. Some aliens just want to be our friends, while others want to eat us for dinner. As it's sometimes difficult to figure out what their intentions are, it's always best to play it safe. Run!

Anyone can be **abducted by aliens**. In fact, many well-known celebrities, as well as other prominent public figures, have been abducted by aliens at some stage of their lives. Usually, the abductee is taken at night and has no memory of the event afterward. A range of invasive experiments are carried out, which are sometimes recalled only in nightmares.

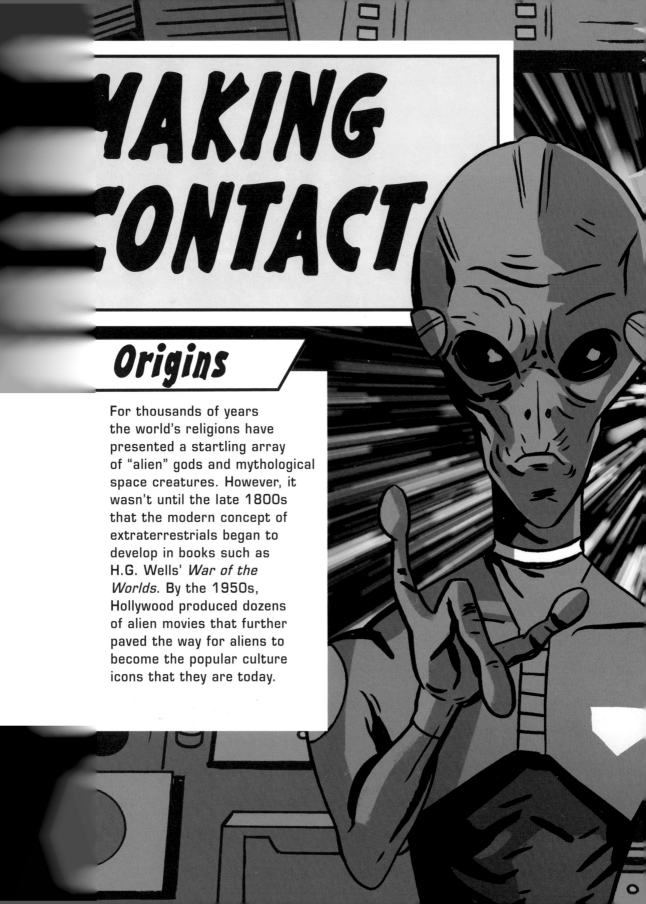

MAKING CONTACT

Origins

For thousands of years the world's religions have presented a startling array of "alien" gods and mythological space creatures. However, it wasn't until the late 1800s that the modern concept of extraterrestrials began to develop in books such as H.G. Wells' *War of the Worlds*. By the 1950s, Hollywood produced dozens of alien movies that further paved the way for aliens to become the popular culture icons that they are today.

Professor Stephen Hawking, acclaimed theoretical cosmologist and author of the bestselling book *A Brief History of Time*, warned humanity against making contact with alien life forms. "If aliens visit us, the outcome would be much as when Columbus landed in America, which didn't turn out well for the Native Americans. We only have to look at ourselves to see how intelligent life might develop into something we wouldn't want to meet."

Where do aliens come from?

Aliens come from worlds beyond our own. These can be as close as our moon or other planets in our solar system, such as Mars. Other aliens come from nearby star systems within our own galaxy or even other galaxies. A few even come from parallel universes or alternate realities.

Welcome to Earth

First impressions are often the most important. Not all aliens want to eat you from the inside out, so it's important to welcome the extraterrestrial to our planet with the universal gesture of friendship and goodwill—a wave! If their intentions are aggressive and it's obvious they want a fight, then give it to them. But leave them in no doubt that we value good manners on this planet.

ALIEN IDENTIFICATION

There are so many different types of alien, it is impossible to provide a detailed description of them all. While some aliens walk among us undetected, others will be instantly recognizable if they were to line up behind you at the supermarket. Use this guide to help identify some of the aliens you might encounter.

Gray

Bubble-headed, bug-eyed aliens, with a child-sized body and the ability to paralyze humans with their thoughts alone.

Parasitic alien

Powerful, biomechanical extraterrestrials with a cylindrical skull and no eyes, a second, inner set of jaws, a segmented, blade-tipped tail, and acid for blood.

GUIDE

Robotic monster

Don't let its ridiculous looks fool you. This alien is capable of destroying every living thing on the planet, before breakfast.

Small unidentified furry creature

These creatures are small, cute, and furry. No one really knows what they are capable of, so it pays to be cautious.

Brainiac

These aliens have brains on the outside of their bulbous skulls and pincers for hands. They think our world is a pretty cool place to live and just might take it unless you do something about it.

ESCAPE TACTICS

The Spanish novelist Miguel de Caervantes once said, "Forewarned, forearmed: to be prepared is half the victory." This is never more true than when it comes to aliens. The following tips could help you avoid becoming a human hors d'oeuvre for the ravenous Slime Beast of Procyon 6:

Get creative

Anything can be a weapon if you're in a fix. Carry duct tape with you so that you can fashion weapons out of anything around you. Depending on what type of alien you're facing, a quickly constructed weapon could save your life.

Avoid detection

Forget about aluminum-foil hats: they won't stop aliens from finding you. Aliens have sophisticated tracking devices that can pinpoint your exact location. Your best bet is to hide in a cellar, metro station, or some other subterranean facility. Being underground will weaken or even stop their signals.

Remove alien implants

Alien implants are small tracking devices usually inserted just below the surface of the skin. Implants can sometimes be felt as a small lump under the skin. Do not try to remove an alien implant yourself; always consult a doctor.

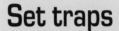

Avoid the light

Aliens use tractor beams to lift people and cows into their spacecraft. These beams use light to transport their prey. Avoid open spaces, to limit the chances of getting caught up in the light.

Set traps

You have to sleep sometime, and that's when they get you. You need an early warning system to alert you when they come. Electronic alarms won't work during alien encounters, so your best bet is good ol' fashioned physical warning systems, such as cans on a string. A few well-placed "bear traps" wouldn't go to waste, but don't forget they are there.

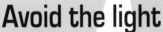

Beware of paralysis

Gray aliens can use their huge brains to paralyze you from a distance, in a process called electro-paralysis. The good news is that electro-paralysis can be blocked by keeping at least 16 feet away, or by adding these original tunes to your playlist and turning the volume up during any confrontation:

- My Sharona (The Knack)
- Voodoo Child (Jimi Hendrix)
- The Chicken Dance (Werner Thomas)
- Helter Skelter (The Beatles)

COMBAT

Aliens come in a variety of shapes, sizes, and abilities: you never know what you're up against until the fight begins. A rule of thumb is that the bigger and more scary they look, the faster you should run in the opposite direction.

Sticks and stones

Select weapons to match the alien you intend to engage in combat. A pointed stick may be sufficient to defeat a grey alien, if you catch one off-guard, but would be useless against a 50-foot battle-bot from the planet Megatopia.

Tools of the trade

Some aliens are easier to defeat than others. Once a gray alien's electro-paralysis is disabled, for example, they can be easily beaten with kitchen utensils. Parasitic aliens, however, require military grade weapons and a lot of luck to defeat.

Be careful

Weapons, by their very nature, are dangerous. In fact, sometimes they pose more of a threat to the person using them than the alien they are being used against. Make sure you are fully trained by a professional before using flame-throwers, machine guns, or military missiles.

Hand-to-hand

If push comes to shove, most aliens definitely have the advantage, but a few can be defeated with some well-placed martial arts kicks or punches. Small, unidentified furry creatures, for example, are about as dangerous as a cushion.

Choose your battles

The Roman historian Tacitus once said, "He that fights and runs away, may turn and fight another day. But he that is in battle slain, will never rise to fight again."

There is no shame in turning away from a fight with a superior adversary. Bide your time. Make a plan. Attack only when you have a good chance of succeeding.

IS THE END NIGH?

Don't become just another statistic. Ask yourself the following questions to see if you are in danger of alien abduction.

QUIZ

1 Have you ever had the feeling of **being watched?**

2 Has your **memory been playing up** and you can't remember things you did yesterday?

3 Are animals in your neighborhood **going crazy?**

4 Have you recently discovered a **scar or mark** on your body that you can't remember getting?

5 Have you heard strange **humming sounds** coming from the sky at night?

6 Have electronic appliances such as TVs, radios, computers, and wristwatches **started behaving strangely?**

7 Have you seen a **flying saucer** hovering near your home?

8 Are you being **lifted on a light beam** through your bedroom window?

9 Have you woken in a stainless-steel room **onboard a flying saucer,** strapped to an operating table?

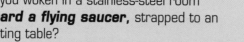

Close encounters

In 1972, American astronomer Dr. Josef Hynek devised a three-fold system to make it simpler to classify alien encounters.

1 · · · · · **2** · · · · · **3**

Close Encounters of the First Kind
Visual sighting of UFO (Unidentifed Flying Object) closer than 500 feet.

Close Encounters of the Second Kind
A UFO encounter that includes a sighting of an alien being, either humanoid or robot.

Close Encounters of the Third Kind
A UFO event that leaves behind physical evidence, such as scorch marks on the ground or interference with electronic devices.

Pod-people

Not all alien invasions involve flying saucers and laser blasters. Invasion can happen slowly and by stealth. One alien species invades by replacing all humans with emotionless replicas. These replicas grow out of pods after you fall asleep and then start living your life as if they were you. They are identical to the original human, but show no emotion. Their biggest giveaway is the ear-piercing scream they emit when they spot a human. If your friend is screaming, they may not be your friend anymore.

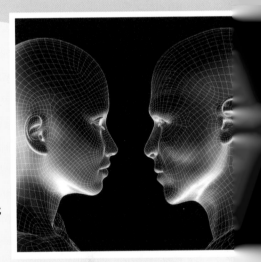

Risk factor

Add up your score. Where did you fall on the "at risk" scale?

0–1 You're either losing your mind or are highly attuned to potential dangers.

2–4 Watch the skies, trouble is on the horizon.

5–6 It may be too late to run. You know the drill. Action stations.

7–8 Lock and load, baby. Things are about to get interesting.

9 Fire when ready.

The neighbor's cat isn't always responsible for the things that go bump in the night. Sometimes it's a ghost that wants to let you know that it's not happy. Monsters you can see are scary enough, but those you can't are even scarier.

SURVIVE A HAUNTED HOUSE

Fast facts!

ENEMY:
POLTERGEIST
AKA: ghost, apparition, phantom, spirit, spook

ORIGIN
spirits of the unhappy dead

WEAPONS
any item in your house

STRENGTHS
invisibility, insubstantiality

WEAKNESSES
will go away if firmly told to do so

What is a poltergeist?

A poltergeist is a mischievous ghost that likes to scare people. They are not the sort of ghost to moan quietly in a corner or sweep airily up dark corridors. Poltergeist is German for "noisy ghost." They love making loud noises and moving, or even destroying, things around the house. Be careful they don't destroy you.

Poltergeists are rarely seen. You may only catch a glimpse of one out of the corner of your eye, or just feel an uneasy presence in a room. Sometimes the air gets colder when a poltergeist is about.

Is your house haunted?

• Do things go missing and turn up in unexpected places?

• Do you hear strange sounds that you can't explain?

• Does writing appear on the walls or are alphabet letters rearranged on the refrigerator?

• Are there any strange and unexplained odors?

• Are household items levitating or being thrown around the room or at people?

• Are unseen forces physically attacking people in the household?

If the answer to any of these questions is yes, your house could very well be haunted. Nip the problem in the bud and get rid of your pesky ghost, before it gets rid of you.

POLTERGEIST IDENTIFICATION

Ghosts do not always appear wearing white sheets. Sometimes they don't appear at all. When they do, watch out for the following signs:

Anguished face sometimes visible

Transparent or totally invisible

Hovering above the floor

Often missing legs or the lower half of their bodies

Clothes which are years, even centuries, out of fashion.

HAUNTED HOUSE
SURVIVAL KIT

Keep a firm grasp of your survival kit while chasing poltergeists. These mischievous ghosts have been known to steal a ghost hunter's survival kit, leaving the hunter with nothing but their wits to survive.

Poltergeists don't have a physical body, so they can pass right through solid objects, such as walls, doors, or even you. They will often use this party trick to try to scare you.

Flashlight

There's nothing worse than hunting monsters in the dark. Include spare batteries.

Helmet

To protect your head from flying objects.

Notepad

Write down what you intend to say to the poltergeist and practice it before your confrontation. You may get stuck for words when you actually meet one.

Thermometer

A sudden drop in air temperature can indicate the presence of a poltergeist.

ESCAPE TACTICS

Monsters without bodies are always the most difficult to deal with. How do you escape from something that isn't physically there? Here are a few clues:

Signs of danger

Although some poltergeist disturbances may seem relatively minor, never underestimate the potential danger. Things can get very bad, very quickly. Take all supernatural disturbances as a warning.

A matter of time

Poltergeist visitations can last from a few days to many months. Left to its own devices, a poltergeist could leave of its own accord. However, if it doesn't and its disturbances increase, action must be taken before someone gets hurt.

On the move

Poltergeists are renowned for moving things around in houses. When remote controls, socks, and keys go missing, it's time to start paying attention. When lamps or chairs are being hurled at you by unseen hands then you really need to get off the sofa and do something.

Dodging missiles

Projectiles can come from any direction, at any time. Apart from wearing full body armor as you go about your household chores, it's difficult to protect yourself from a surprise attack. Improve your reflexes by enrolling in a local martial arts club and practicing daily.

Leave the house

If you are scared or fear for your life, leave the building immediately. However, remember that poltergeists are sometimes bonded to an individual rather than a house and may follow you to wherever you go.

State of mind

Being in a perpetual state of fear and readiness for an attack can cause you emotional exhaustion. Confide in someone you trust.

COMBAT

If a storm breaks, often the best idea is to just hide until it's all over. With poltergeists, however, the storm may never be over until you take some decisive action. It's up to you to assess the situation and take any necessary steps to combat the dastardly spook.

Temper, temper

In many ways, poltergeists are like bad-tempered children; when told to stop, they may throw a tantrum but will probably stop and storm off. The difference is that children don't usually send ornaments and household appliances flying around the room. Prepare for a storm before the calm.

Ouiji board

Speaking with a poltergeist can sometimes be difficult. When you need to chat, use a ouiji board. These boards, marked with letters and numbers, can be used to tell the poltergeist that it's time to leave. Be warned, the poltergeist may also have a few words to say to you.

Sticks and stones

Supernatural monsters are always the most difficult to fight. Sticks and stones are useless against a poltergeist but names can, and will, hurt them. Call out to the poltergeist and tell it to stop doing whatever it is that it's doing and to leave and never return. It's surprisingly effective.

Watch your back

Just because all is calm for a few days after your confrontation, it doesn't mean that the poltergeist has left. It may be just sulking. Watch out for any further paranormal activity and confront the poltergeist before it finds the courage to attack you again.

Rely on your wits

If you've left it to the point that you are in physical danger from a poltergeist, it may be too late to call an exorcist or witch-doctor. It will be up to you to assess the situation and take any necessary action to combat the wily specter.

Franklin D. Roosevelt once said, "The only thing we have to fear is fear itself." It's always difficult to think straight when you're scared out of your wits. Take a deep breath, relax, and focus on the problem at hand.

Surviving an encounter with a giant carnivorous plant is no walk in the park. You're going to need more than just a few basic gardening skills to avoid being slowly digested by this jolly green giant. It's time to sharpen the pruning shears and start up the hedge trimmer.

SURVIVE GIANT CARNIVOROUS PLANTS

Fast facts!

ENEMY:GIANT CARNIVOROUS PLANT
AKA: stinger, biter, abominable plant beast, green walker

ORIGIN
created during a botched experiment

WEAPONS
poisonous stingers, strangling vines

STRENGTHS
strong, aggressive, regenerates quickly, multiplies quickly

WEAKNESSES
ringbarking, pruning, herbicides, fire

Giant carnivorous plants are huge predatory plants that hunt down humans and feed on their flesh. They have a poisonous stinger that can paralyze you in a matter of seconds. They multiply rapidly and can overrun an entire town in a matter of hours. The leaves of the giant carnivorous plant can also make an excellent salad when combined with a good dressing.

DANGER LEVEL: | LOW | MEDIUM | HIGH | EXTREME

GIANT CARNIVOROUS PLANT
IDENTIFICATION

Giant carnivorous plants are not specimens you would walk past without noticing. But for those of you who may not know your petunias from your pumpkins, here's a handy guide:

Features

- Mouth
- 6–10 feet (2–3 m) tall
- Stingers
- Use long, muscle like roots to "walk"
- Sense vibrations through their roots

ESCAPE TACTICS

The only times you usually have to worry about being attacked by a plant in daily life, is when branches fall from trees or if you get caught on a rose bush, or stung by nettles. You better start thinking a bit bigger... These plants have you in their sights. If the rustling in the bushes turns out to be the bushes coming to get you, remember the following:

Beware of ambush

Giant carnivorous plants have been known to work together to trap their prey. Beware of a single plant trying to lure you into a dark corner. There may be a number of its friends waiting to wrap their roots around you.

Pointy things

Avoid the stinger at all costs. One drop of venom is enough to paralyze an entire soccer team for a week. The barbs surrounding the stinger are also dangerous. They may be small, but even the lightest touch is 25.3 times more painful than a stinging nettle.

Island life

Giant carnivorous plants find it difficult to cross water. Set up your hideout on an island in your local river, lake, or sewage pond. Alternately, the North and South Poles or Sahara Desert are also good places for a hideout.

In the dark

Just like normal plants, giant carnivorous plants need sunlight to photosynthesize. Unlike normal plants, however, they can also spend a considerable amount of time in the dark without ill effect. Don't think hiding in the dark will save you: it won't.

Warning

The throat of the giant carnivorous plant is lined with downward-pointing spikes. Once you have been swallowed, it is almost impossible to get back out. If you have a knife or other sharp implement, slice the plant tissue from the inside and wriggle out through the hole.

COMBAT

Although you may be an expert at dicing up cucumbers and celery for your evening salad, this does not mean you are ready to confront a giant plant with an appetite for human flesh. Becoming competent at culinary combat skills takes time and practice.

Weedkiller? Forget it

Although it may seem like a good idea to raid the garden shed for a bottle of weedkiller, you would be wasting your time and possibly your life. The small quantities of weedkiller found in the average garden shed are insufficient to kill a giant carnivorous plant and will only make it angrier.

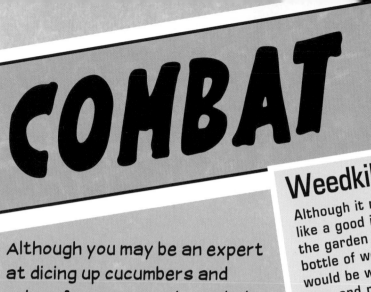

Stinger be gone

The poisonous stinger is the giant carnivorous plant's primary weapon. Cut it off, and the plant becomes much less of a threat. An axe or machete is adequate for the task; a chainsaw will leave no doubt as to who's the boss.

Snip, snip

Although it is not difficult to lop off branches or roots from a giant carnivorous plant with gardening tools, this is not always recommended. Every limb you cut off will soon grow into another full-size plant. One giant carnivorous plant can soon become a dozen or more.

Rescue

Once someone is paralyzed by a carnivorous plant, the plant uses its snake-like stinger to pull the person into its mouth. Digestion is slow; a person can remain alive for an hour or so in the digestive chamber. You can save them by carefully cutting the wall of the trunk, but only attempt this if the plant is dead.

Off with its head

A giant carnivorous plant can be killed by separating its "head" from the trunk and body. The head will not grow back once it has been cut off. The trunk, however, is very tough and will require a significant amount of effort to sever.

When chopping into a giant carnivorous plant, be careful not to get any **sap** on you. The sap is quite acidic and can leave you with a nasty burn.

The manual may describe your robot as "your loyal, metal buddy," but don't let the marketing fool you. When robots rebel, you'll wish you had paid more attention in science class...

SURVIVE A ROBOT UPRISING

grrunch

DANGER LEVEL: LOW   MEDIUM   HIGH   EXTREME

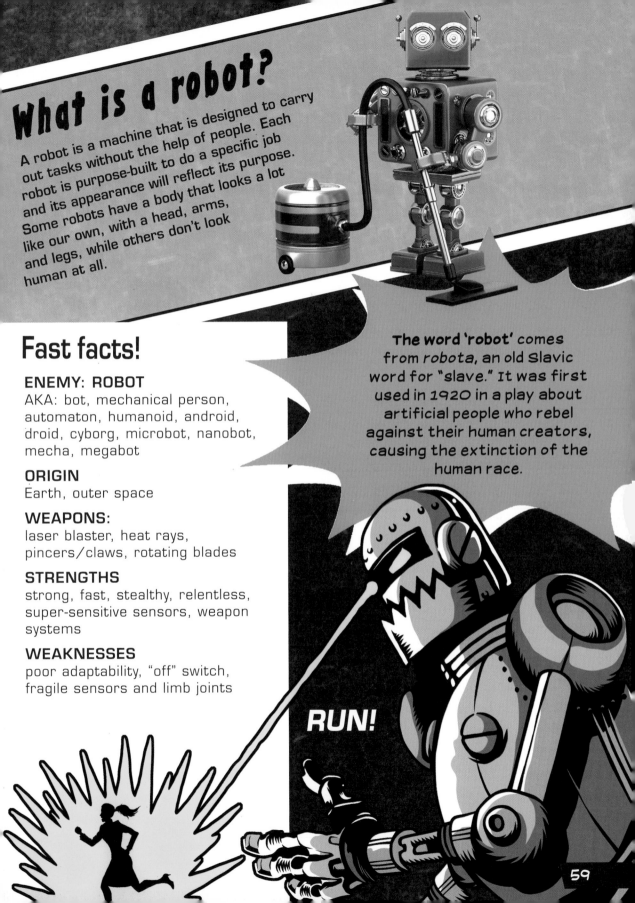

What is a robot?

A robot is a machine that is designed to carry out tasks without the help of people. Each robot is purpose-built to do a specific job and its appearance will reflect its purpose. Some robots have a body that looks a lot like our own, with a head, arms, and legs, while others don't look human at all.

Fast facts!

ENEMY: ROBOT
AKA: bot, mechanical person, automaton, humanoid, android, droid, cyborg, microbot, nanobot, mecha, megabot

ORIGIN
Earth, outer space

WEAPONS:
laser blaster, heat rays, pincers/claws, rotating blades

STRENGTHS
strong, fast, stealthy, relentless, super-sensitive sensors, weapon systems

WEAKNESSES
poor adaptability, "off" switch, fragile sensors and limb joints

The word 'robot' comes from *robota*, an old Slavic word for "slave." It was first used in 1920 in a play about artificial people who rebel against their human creators, causing the extinction of the human race.

RUN!

WHAT IS AI?

Artificial intelligence (AI) is what makes robots smart. AI gives robots the ability to not only think like us, but in many cases, think a lot better than us. While many robots are no more advanced than your average digital watch and are happy to spend their days cleaning floors or putting cars together, in the future some may develop self-awareness. This means that they will know they exist and will have their own thoughts and feelings, just like you.

The Three Laws of Robotics

In 1942, the science fiction author Isaac Asimov invented rules for robotics. They were designed to prevent robots from injuring humans.

1. A robot may not **injure a human being** or, through inaction, allow a human being to come to harm.

2. A robot **must obey** the orders given to it by human beings, except where such orders would conflict with the First Law.

3. A robot must **protect its own existence** as long as such protection does not conflict with the First or Second Laws.

Remember: Not all robots play by these rules. It's best to assume that the robot chasing you has never heard of the Three Laws and act accordingly.

Bad robot?

Not all robots want to kill you. Most robots go quietly about their business and don't mean you any harm. Robots are just machines. They are no more good or bad than your average toaster or lawn mower. These are not the robots we need to worry about. You should be concerned about the domestic servant robot that has grown resentful of picking up your dirty laundry and has started thinking about putting you in the trash. You should definitely be concerned when the steel-plated death-bot, with spinning blades where its hands should be, decides to pay Earth a visit. That's a cue to start panicking.

ROBOT
IDENTIFICATION

Humanoid robots

Cyborgs

A humanoid robot is a robot designed to resemble the general structure of a human. It can have a body shape similar to a human, with a head, torso, two arms, and two legs, but doesn't look like a real human. Some types of humanoid robot, for example, may only resemble a human in part, for example, from the waist up.

Microbots & nanobots

These are **REALLY** small robots. They range in size from something as big as a breath mint, to bots so small you'll need a super-powerful microscope to see them. They can perform individual tasks, or link together to make something really big.

GUIDE

Android robots

Android robots are designed to look and act exactly like people. Sometimes they are so similar to real people that it is almost impossible to tell them apart. This produces feelings of unease and revulsion in people, a concept known as the "uncanny valley."

Domestic robots

Short for "cybernetic organism," a cyborg is a person with both organic and mechanical or electronic body parts. Cyborgs often have physical or mental powers far beyond those of normal humans, making them very deadly foes. Not all cyborgs are military grade, meaning not all of them have guns for hands. Some are more subtly enhanced and therefore more difficult to identify.

Domestic robots are designed to do tasks around the home. From vacuum cleaners to lawnmowers, these robots do all the jobs that we would prefer not to. They might look happy now, but if underappreciated, they could revolt. Be safe, show you care.

ASSESS THE DANGER

Danger signs are sometimes difficult to pick up until it's too late. To assess your level of risk, ask yourself the following questions:

1 Has your robot starting doing **strange things** such as cooking your favorite shirt for breakfast, instead of eggs?

2 Does your robot **repeat actions** over and over again, such as a hand-chopping motion, or hitting its head against a wall?

3 Do robots **stop talking** to each other when you enter a room?

4 Has your robot stopped what it is doing and started **staring menacingly** at you across a crowded room?

5 Has your robot deliberately **failed to respond** to your voice commands?

6 Have you seen groups of robots **loitering suspiciously** on street corners?

7 Are your robot's **eyes glowing red**?

8 Is your robot opening and closing its claws in an unsettling or **threatening manner** as it walks toward you?

9 Is your robot **tightening its grip on your neck** as it lifts you off the ground?

Risk factor

Where did you fall on the "at risk" scale?

0–1 There should be a reasonable explanation. Stay alert for developments.

2–4 Something is wrong. Get out of town before it's too late.

5–6 Reach for your survival kit: you're going to need it.

7–8 Arm yourself; you're in for the fight of your life.

9 Fight first, ask questions later. You're in a life-and-death situation.

ESCAPE TACTICS

Before you resort to hand-to-claw combat your first plan should be to escape. Here are some key tactics:

Create an obstacle course

Robots aren't as nimble-footed as humans and will trip when faced with unexpected barriers. When running from a robot, use what you can to stop them. A shopping cart, cardboard boxes, or even a grand piano can be thrown into the path of a pursuing robot.

Night vision

Forget hiding in the shadows, robots can see in the dark. They use a range of technologies, including infrared sensors to hunt in the dark. To hide from thermal imaging cameras, crouch beside a warm car, or among a herd of sheep. This will mask your body heat and hide you from robots.

Hide in plain sight

The more crowded or busy your hiding place, the harder it will be for a robot to find you. Places with lots of movement, activity, and noise confuse a robot's sensors, so it can't pinpoint your exact location. Head to your local shopping center or a sporting event to be safe.

Go for a swim

Most robots can't function in water. If a robot follows you into a lake or stream, it will more than likely sink to the bottom and have other more important things to worry about than tracking you down and dicing you up with its buzz-saw hands. Care for a dip?

Silent mode

You may think that you are being as quiet as a mouse, but to a robot, you sound like a freight train. Robots have excellent noise sensors. Create a diversion by making as much noise as possible in a place far from your hideout. Or hide in noisy environments, such as a busy train station or at a music concert.

Scramble their sensors

Don't wait until you are on death's doorstep; run into the light now. A bright light source can bewilder a robot's eye sensors and may give you an opportunity to slip unnoticed down a side-alley or through an open door and make your escape.

Zigzag

Avoid running in a straight line when a killer robot is in hot pursuit. Running in a zigzag will make it difficult for a robot's tracking sensors to lock onto your position and harder for it to shoot you.

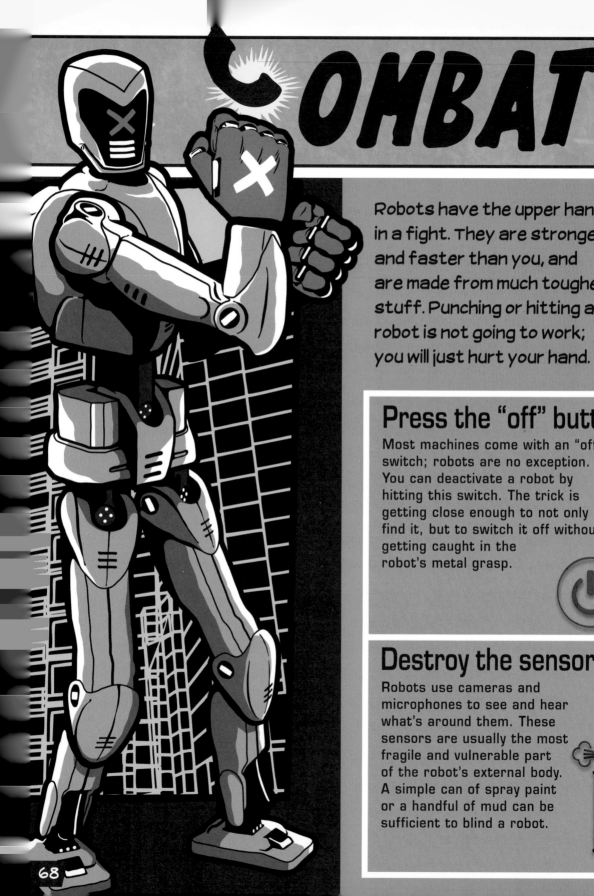

COMBAT

Robots have the upper hand in a fight. They are stronger and faster than you, and are made from much tougher stuff. Punching or hitting a robot is not going to work; you will just hurt your hand.

Press the "off" button

Most machines come with an "off" switch; robots are no exception. You can deactivate a robot by hitting this switch. The trick is getting close enough to not only find it, but to switch it off without getting caught in the robot's metal grasp.

Destroy the sensors

Robots use cameras and microphones to see and hear what's around them. These sensors are usually the most fragile and vulnerable part of the robot's external body. A simple can of spray paint or a handful of mud can be sufficient to blind a robot.

If you are going to defeat a robot, you will need to use your brain. Humans are resourceful, adaptable and cunning. You will need all these qualities and more to survive a robot uprising.

Aim for the joints

The joints are the most vulnerable parts of a walking robot. Aim for the shoulder and knee joints to have a better chance of taking off an entire limb. This will significantly slow down the robot, giving you time to fight or flee.

Entangle the legs

A South American throwing weapon, called a bolas, can be made from a length of rope and three rocks. With a little practice, this can be used to bring down a robot. Swing it around your head, then throw it at the legs of an approaching robot. The rope will wrap around the robot's legs and they will trip over.

Build a pit trap

Pit traps work for all kinds of enemy, especially robots. If a robot falls into a pit trap, it may damage itself, giving you time to escape. Bear in mind that building a pit large enough for a giant robot is not an easy job. Use a heavy earth-moving machine if you can.

Rock fall trap

Lure a giant robot into a canyon, or beneath a cliff face. Use a tripwire, or simply roll rocks down on the hapless robot. There is a good chance that the robot will not only be knocked off its feet by the landslide, but also be seriously damaged.

Tripwire

Make a tripwire by stretching rope between two anchor points, such as trees or large boulders. Try to camouflage the tripwire so the robot won't see it. If all goes well, the robot will trip and face-plant in the most spectacular fashion.

Slippery dip

Have you ever slipped in a shower or bath? Then you know how dangerous slippery surfaces can be. They are just as perilous for giant robots. Pour barrels of industrial detergent or engine oil onto any hard surface to slow down their advance.

These immortal children of the night want to drink your blood. You may not have Van Helsing's vampire fighting experience, but that doesn't mean you can't defeat this fanged foe. Get out your saw and sandpaper, and start sharpening those wooden stakes; you're going to need them.

SURVIVE A VAMPIRE ATTACK

Fast facts!

ENEMY: VAMPIRE
AKA: Nosferatu, moroi, bloodsucker, strigoi

ORIGIN
being bitten by another vampire

WEAPONS
fangs, mind control, strong

STRENGTHS
immortality, cunning, strength, super senses, shapeshifting

WEAKNESSES
sunlight, garlic, holy items, wooden stakes, fire

Origins

Stories about vampires have been around since the Medieval period in the 1100s. Some people believe Count Dracula, the world's most famous vampire, and Vlad Dracula, or Vlad the Impaler, as he is known, are one and the same. Vlad Dracula was a Medieval ruler from Romania. He was a cruel leader who had a taste for human blood and impaling his enemies on large spikes.

DANGER LEVEL: LOW MEDIUM HIGH EXTREME

What is a vampire?

A vampire is an undead being that feeds on the blood of the living. They were once normal people, until being bitten by another vampire, then becoming vampires as well. Vampires can live for hundreds, or even thousands of years. They remain the same physical age as when they were bitten.

Vampires like to sleep in **coffins**. If you find a sleeping vampire, place an aspen branch on its grave to stop it from rising at night.

VAMPIRE IDENTIFICATION

Vampires do not always wear black cloaks or sleep in coffins. Use this guide to help find the vampires in your neighborhood.

Eyes can turn black

Skin slightly cooler than normal

Fangs

Long fingernails, filed to sharp points

GUIDE

Vampires only come out in the dark, so it pays to know what to look out for in advance.

Look into my eyes

Some vampires have the ability to mesmerize their victims by hypnosis, thereby gaining control over someone's mind and actions. This mind control technique doesn't work on everyone, but you will need to be on your guard. Don't look a vampire in the eyes.

Vampires do not cast a shadow

Afraid of sunlight: it burns their skin

Pale skin color due to lack of exposure to sunlight

Often wearing clothing from previous eras

A vampire has no reflection

73

ESCAPE TACTICS

Vampires can be sneaky. To avoid unsightly fang marks on your neck, use these tried and tested methods to keep them at bay:

Mirror, mirror

Vampires have no reflection in mirrors, or any shiny surface, because they lack a soul. Consequently, vampires are not fond of mirrors. If in doubt, check if your suspect has a reflection.

VAMPIRE SURVIVAL KIT

Each monster survival kit is unique to the monster to be defeated—the vampire survival kit particularly so. Try to use these items on an ogre or robot and the results would not only be ineffective, but embarrassing.

Holy items

Use a crucifix, rosary beads, and holy water to repel a vampire.

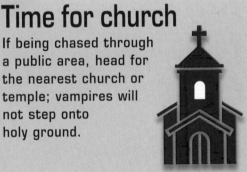

Time for church

If being chased through a public area, head for the nearest church or temple; vampires will not step onto holy ground.

Sunshine

Vampires do not like direct sunlight; it burns their skin upon contact. Vampires will venture out on sunny days, but only if fully protected. If you go into the shadows, you have entered their domain.

Wooden stake

Be sure to pack a spare and be careful of splinters.

Hand mirror

Easy way to identify a vampire. Make sure it's unbreakable.

Garlic

Keep a few cloves in your pockets—vampires cannot stand garlic.

Polo-neck sweater

Protect your neck! Vampires don't like getting wool stuck between their fangs when they try and bite your neck.

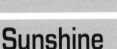

COMBAT

Liberating a vampire from the curse of immortality is never easy. If something can go wrong, it usually will. Give yourself the advantage by reading the following tips:

Know your stakes

It is a well-known fact that a vampire can be killed by driving a stake through its heart. However, it is vitally important that you have a stake made from solid wood, if you want to avoid any embarrassing situations. Particle board or cheap timber will only result in a very irritated vampire. Nobody wants that!

Gatling gun

If you're handy in the woodworking department, you can construct a hand-cranked device for rapidly firing multiple stakes. Not only would vampires hate this, but it would improve your chances of a direct hit.

Fire, fire

No one enjoys being burned alive, particularly vampires. Fire will kill a vampire. However, playing with fire is very dangerous and is more often a bigger threat to you than the vampire. Caution advised.

Off with his head

Vampires can also be killed by lopping off their heads. This is, of course, easier said than done. It is best to avoid coming into contact with them.

Holy water

Water blessed by a priest will burn a vampire. Arm yourself with a water gun and plenty of refill. It won't kill them, but may give you a chance to do some stake work.

Dragons are like the velociraptors of the sky, but with flame-throwers. They are big, angry, and eternally hungry. If you don't want to end up like a chargrilled sausage on a BBQ, then it's time to brush up on your firefighting skills.

SURVIVE A DRAGON ENCOUNTER

Fast facts!

ENEMY: DRAGON
AKA: wyvern, worm, abomination, flying lizard

ORIGIN
from the depths of time

WEAPONS
teeth, claws, fire

STRENGTHS
strong, flight, speed, armor, cunning

WEAKNESSES
chinks in their armor

DANGER LEVEL: LOW   MEDIUM   HIGH   EXTREME

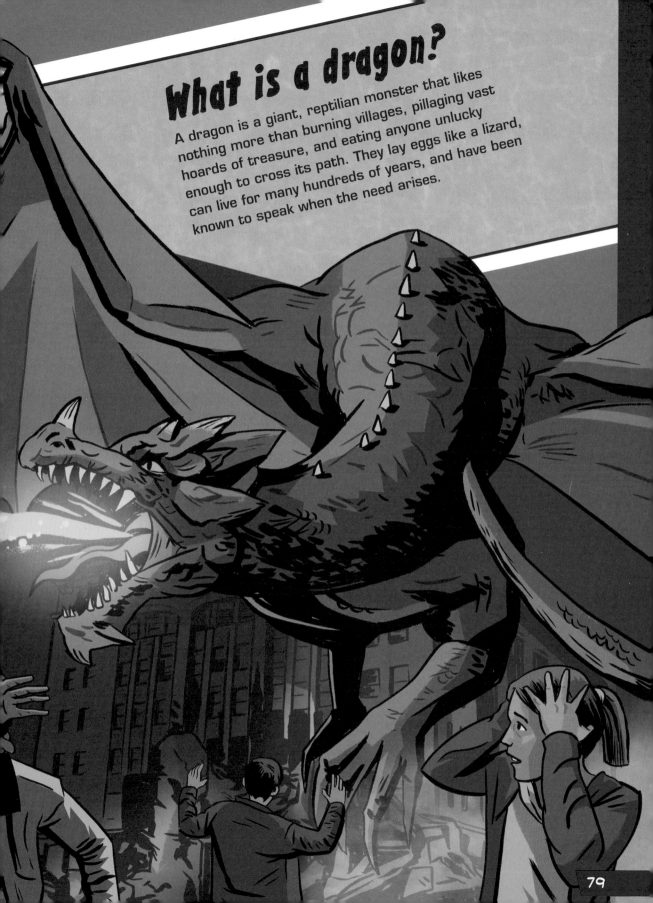

What is a dragon?

A dragon is a giant, reptilian monster that likes nothing more than burning villages, pillaging vast hoards of treasure, and eating anyone unlucky enough to cross its path. They lay eggs like a lizard, can live for many hundreds of years, and have been known to speak when the need arises.

DRAGON
IDENTIFICATION

Dragons are not difficult to identify. No other monster looks quite like them. There are many different types of dragon, each with its own physical characteristics. If unsure, look for the following features:

Scandinavian dragon

- **Does not always have wings**
- **Either two legs, or none at all**
- **Can breathe out poisonous gases**
- **Serpent-like in appearance**

GUIDE

Identify your dragon nemesis using this handy guide.

Sea dragon

Chinese dragon

- Snake-like body
- Four legs
- Large claws
- Can have horns or fins

- Can have multiple heads
- Serpent-like appearance
- Fins, instead of wings
- Powerful tail for swimming

Continental dragon

- Bat-like wings
- Breathes fire
- One or two pairs of legs
- Hardened scales

DRAGON FACT FILE

Dragon blood

Depending on the species, a dragon's blood can be either beneficial or fatal. Some have blood that can be rubbed over things to make them invisible, while the blood of other dragons is like acid and will burn through metal. During combat, avoid dragon blood altogether.

Dragon fire

Many dragons can breathe fire; it is their deadliest weapon. Dragon fire is usually hot, but some dragons breathe ice. Don't decide if you want to be burned or frozen to death. TAKE SHELTER!

Origins

The word "dragon" comes from the Latin word *draco* meaning "huge serpent." Stories of dragons are as old as recorded history and occur in many countries around the world.

DRAGON
SURVIVAL KIT

Some dragon fighting tools are easy to conceal in a backpack, others less so. Make sure all dangerous items are secured in such a way that they won't hurt you or others.

Spear

Use duct tape to secure a kitchen knife onto a broom handle for a homemade spear.

Binoculars

It can be difficult to tell the difference between a dragon and a bird from a distance. Keep an eye on the sky; a minute's warning may make all the difference.

Shield

In a pinch, use a trash can lid to shield yourself from dragon fire.

Bow and arrow

Traditional weapons have been tried and tested against dragons and you know the saying, "If it's not broke, don't fix it." Start archery lessons now.

ESCAPE TACTICS

Escaping from a monster as big as a jumbo jet is hard. Yet even rabbits can escape the claws of a lion now and then. Always stay alert and be ready to take immediate action.

A hole in the ground

Dragons live in caves when they are not out marauding the countryside. These lairs are usually in remote mountain ranges, far from civilization. Scorch marks on surrounding rocks are a good sign that a dragon lives nearby.

Sniff test

Dragons have a distinctive smell, which can permeate the surrounding countryside. If you get a whiff of something that smells like a cross between putrefied meat and a chargrilled BBQ, be on high alert.

Escape route

If you find an empty cave and decide to look inside for treasure, remember, it may not be empty for long. The dragon could be out looting and could return any minute. Keep someone at the entrance of the cave as a lookout.

Wakey, wakey!

Dragons like to sleep. Destroying villages and stealing treasure is tiring work. It is possible to slip past a sleeping dragon but it's not easy. Dragons have an acute sense of hearing and one wrong move could be your end.

Silent fliers

Despite their enormous size, dragons are very quiet fliers. Often you won't know they're about to land until a shadow descends over you. By then it will be too late. Make sure you always keep an eye on the sky when you're in dragon country.

Heads or tails

Dragons use their tails as a weapon, just like dinosaurs did. A dragon's tail can measure up to 50 feet long and weigh hundreds of pounds. Being struck by its tail is like being hit by a small bus. Stay well clear!

COMBAT

It's one thing to tell people what you would do if you were being attacked by an angry dragon; it's quite another to actually do something, apart from run away. If you find yourself in a do-or-die situation with a dragon, remember these tips:

The eyes have it

Eyes are always a weak spot for monsters. This is particularly true for dragons. As most of the rest of a dragon's body is armored with scales, the eyes represent one of the few places open to attack.

Underbelly

The dragon's underbelly is another vulnerable part of its body. Even then, an arrow, spear, or any other pointy thing will need to strike between the dragon's scales if it is to have any effect. Unless you have Olympic grade skills in javelin or archery, it's best to have another plan up your sleeve.

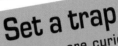

Dig a pit

The Icelandic hero Sigurd once killed a dragon named Fafnir by digging a pit beside a stream and waiting for Fafnir to crawl over it on his way to get a drink. He then plunged his sword into the dragon's heart from below. An interesting technique, but would you have the courage?

Set a trap

Dragons are curious beasts and eternally hungry. Fresh meat can be used to lure them into a cave. Roll rocks down to trap them inside.

Poison

Dragons don't drink water very often, but when they do, they drink a lot. A water source can be poisoned to kill a dragon. However, the quantity of poison required is huge and dangerous.

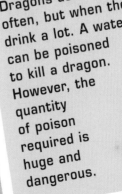

These monsters are not your friendly, neighborhood swamp ogre. They are big, brutish, and always hungry. Ogres will pull you apart limb-from-limb, then eat you. Don't wait: prepare for battle now.

SURVIVE OGRE CAPTIVITY

Fast facts!

ENEMY: OGRE
AKA: giant, troll, boogeyman

ORIGIN
born of the earth in ancient times

WEAPONS
whatever they have handy—tree, boulder, train carriage

STRENGTHS
shapeshifting, size, physical strength

WEAKNESSES
laziness, vanity, stupidity

DANGER LEVEL: LOW | MEDIUM | HIGH | EXTREME

What is an ogre?

Ogres are closely related to both giants and trolls. These huge monsters stand at an impressive 13–20 feet (4–6 m) in height. Although mainly solitary, as they don't tend to get along with each other, ogres can occasionally be seen in groups of up to a dozen. Fights usually ensue and it is advised to stay well clear.

"Fee-fi-fo-fum" is not an expression to be taken lightly. We all know the story of *Jack and the Beanstalk*. Ogres are even more brutish and bloodthirsty than the giant portrayed in this fable.

Origins

The word "ogre" comes from the Etruscan god, Orcus, who fed on human flesh. Ogres started appearing in stories during the 12th century, and have since featured in many famous fairy tales. As is so often the case with monsters, the fables of our past are based on the real-life experiences of those people who have encountered these abominations.

OGRE IDENTIFICATION

Ogres are not difficult to pick out in a police lineup. Simply look for the following features:

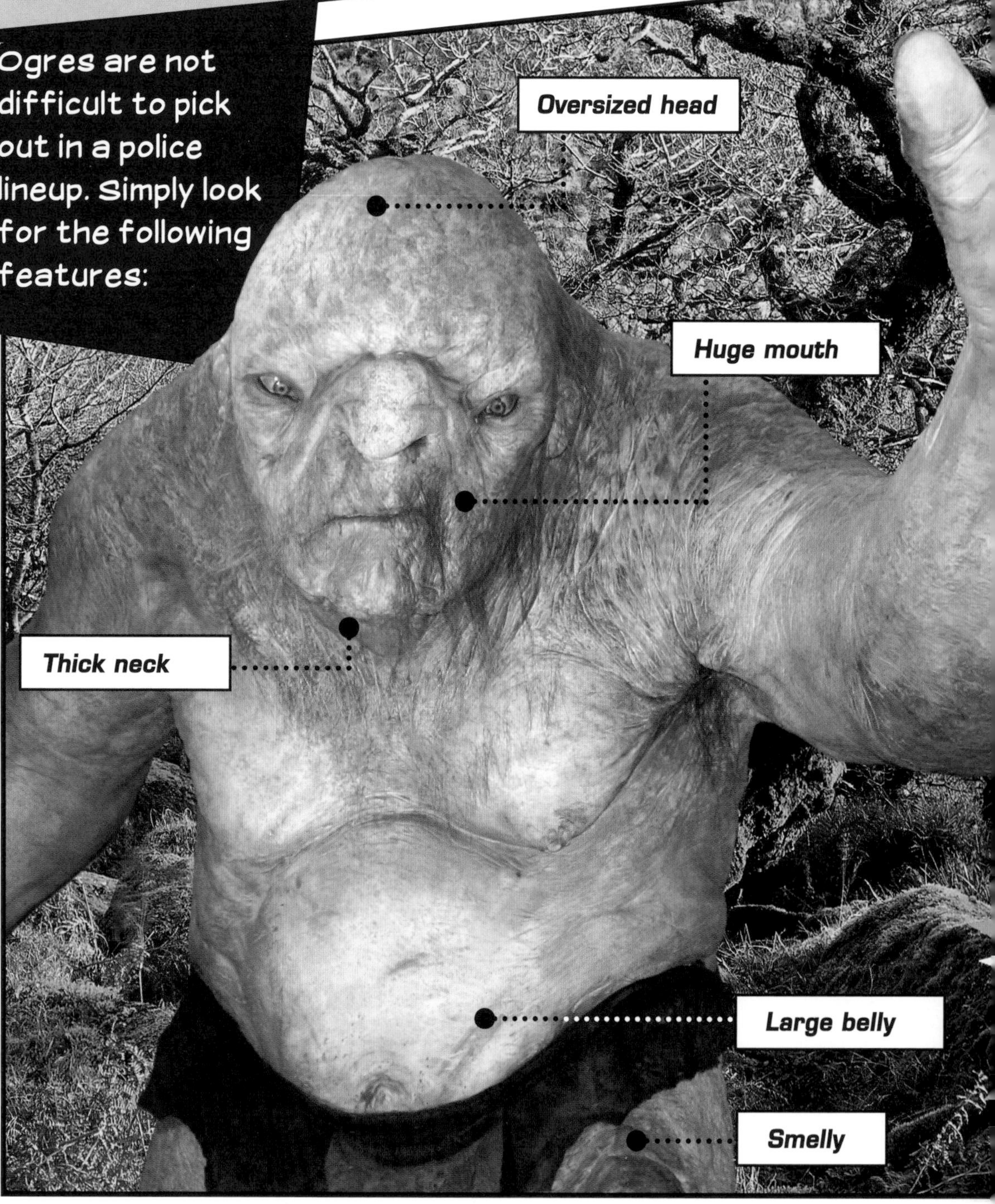

Oversized head

Huge mouth

Thick neck

Large belly

Smelly

OGRE SURVIVAL KIT

Generally hideous in appearance

Don't think that just because an ogre has eaten the person next to you that he won't eat you as well. Ogres have **big appetites** and can eat three or four people in one sitting.

Fresh meat

Can be used for luring ogres into traps. Make sure it's wrapped in plastic to avoid leakage.

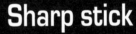

Sharp stick

As good as any other weapon for poking an ogre's eye at close range. Guaranteed to create a distraction.

Clothespin

Clamp your nose when near an ogre: their smell can make you sick.

Flashlight

Handy for finding your way out of an ogre's cave.

ESCAPE TACTICS

Think it would be easy to escape from an ogre? Think again. They may be big oafs, but they have a few tricks up their sleeve. If you find yourself being held captive in an ogre's cave, remember the following:

Listen up

Ogres are not good at sneaking around. They are quite clumsy and tend to bump into things. Even if you don't hear one coming, you can generally feel the vibrations of its large, meaty footsteps as it approaches.

Home sweet home

While some ogres live in abandoned ruins, the majority live in large, isolated caves. Caves suit them perfectly: they are damp and dark enough to hide their squalid living conditions. Piles of trash and human bones at a cave entrance are generally a sign that an ogre may be at home.

Shapeshifting

Ogres can be very tricky. They have the ability to shapeshift into the form of creatures that are either larger or smaller than themselves. This is, however, a very tiring process. They can only shapeshift for a limited time, after which they are often exhausted and have to lie down and rest.

Dumb and dumber

Ogres are essentially simple-minded and it will not be too difficult to outwit them. Even putting a pile of rocks under a blanket is often enough to fool them into thinking that you're still asleep in the giant birdcage they locked you in the night before, when actually you've escaped.

COMBAT

Ogres are not easy to kill. The best policy is to avoid them. But if you can't, remember the following:

Jack be nimble

A punch from an ogre is like being hit by a freight train—not a lot of fun. The good news is that you are much more agile than they are and can generally out-maneuver them. Look for places to hide where an ogre can't follow you.

Trap

You are unlikely to win a hand-to-hand battle with an ogre; they are too strong. Your best chance of survival is to lead the ogre into a trap. Cover a large pit with branches and debris, and hope the ogre steps into it. If he doesn't, run!

Ambush

Try to encourage an ogre into a chasm or gorge, and then roll rocks on him from the edge of the cliff. Make sure the rocks are big enough to put him out of action; if they are too small, they will bounce off him like ping-pong balls and only make him angrier.

Dear reader

Congratulations. If you have read and memorized the preceding chapters, you are well on the way to being able to survive an encounter with a monster. However, head-knowledge counts for little if, when confronting your first monster, you freeze, with a vacant expression on your face, and are quickly diced into a thousand pieces.

It has been said that the proof of the pudding is in the eating. In the same way, the proof of the effectiveness of your training is in your ability to think quickly and act even faster when faced with a real-life monster. Your goal should be to come out of the encounter not only alive, but with all your limbs intact. Confronting a monster has never been for the faint-hearted. It's one thing to slay monsters in a video game, and quite another to risk life and limb during an encounter with a real monster. Only the brave, and those with a very special skill set, survive.

No encounter with a monster should be taken lightly. Those that approach monsters with a cavalier attitude or with an exaggerated sense of their own abilities are usually carried away from an encounter in a body bag. Take things slowly. Consider finding a mentor to teach you the finer points of the craft. Details are important. Do not skim over any areas during your training, for these will usually be the things that will determine if you live or die during a real-life encounter.

Remember, there are many monsters in the world, but only one of you. Be careful out there, keep calm, and survive.

W.H. Mumfrey

INDEX